VOLUME 4

SING WITH THE C

Classic Hits

Exclusive Distributors:
Music Sales Limited
14–15 Berners Street, London W1T 3LJ, UK.

Order No. HLE90003826
ISBN 978-1-84938-041-6

Cover design by Chloë Alexander
Printed in the USA

Your Guarantee of Quality
As publishers, we strive to produce every book to the highest commercial standards.
The book has been carefully designed to minimise awkward page turns and to make playing from it a real pleasure.
Throughout, the printing and binding have been planned to ensure a sturdy, attractive publication which should give years of enjoyment.
If your copy fails to meet our high standards, please inform us and we will gladly replace it.

www.musicsales.com

TITLE	PAGE	CD TRACK
All You Need Is Love The Beatles	4	1
At The Hop Danny & The Juniors	10	2
Good Vibrations The Beach Boys	22	3
The Great Pretender The Platters	15	4
I'm A Believer The Monkees	28	5
Imagine John Lennon	34	6
Rock Around The Clock Bill Haley & His Comets	38	7
Under The Boardwalk The Drifters	42	8

All You Need Is Love

Arranged by
ALAN BILLINGSLEY

Words and Music by JOHN LENNON
and PAUL McCARTNEY

Ah
16
Noth - in' you can say, but you can learn how to play the game, it's

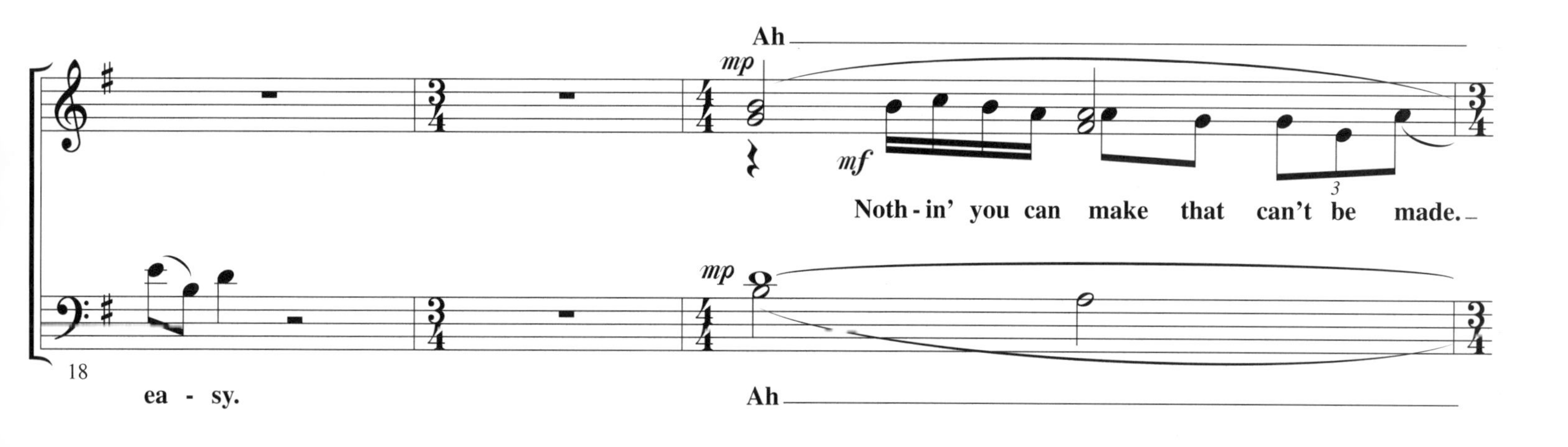
Ah
mp
mf
Noth - in' you can make that can't be made.
18
mp
ea - sy.
Ah

Ah
No one you can save that can't be saved.
21
Ah

Ah
Unis. f
Noth - in' you can do, but you can learn how to be you in time; it's
Unis. f
24
Ah
it's

ea - sy.
All you need is love.
26
All you need is love.
All you need is love,
30
love;
love is all you need.
33
Ah
f
div.
Noth - in' you can know that is - n't known.
Ah
f
Noth - in' you can know that is - n't known.
36
Ah
Noth - in' you can see that is - n't shown.
Ah
Noth - in' you can see that is - n't shown.
38

Ah
No - where you can be that is - n't where you're meant to be; it's
Ah
No - where you can be that is - n't where you're meant to be; it's
40

ea - sy.
All you need is love.
42

All you need is love.
All you need is love,
46

love;
love is all you need.
49

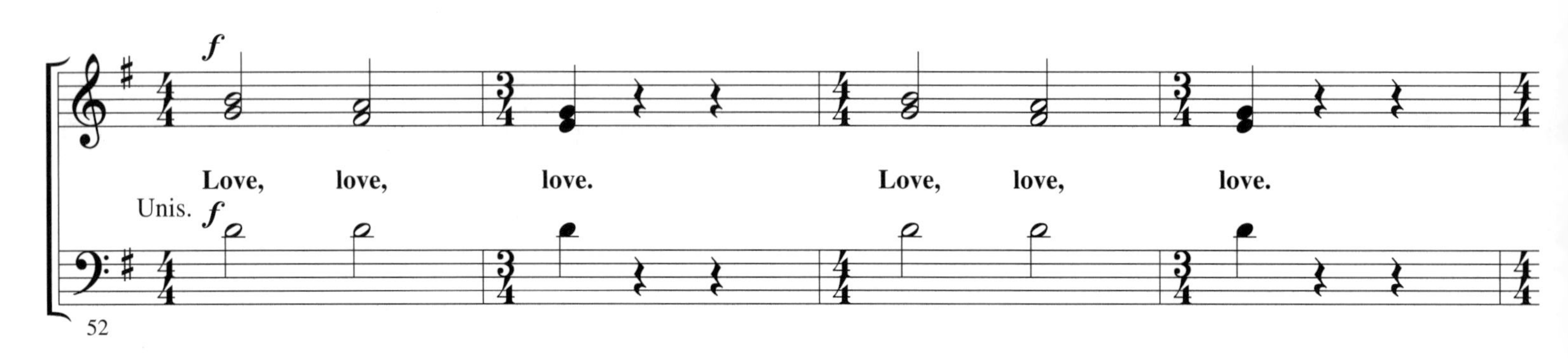
f
Love, love, love. Love, love, love.
Unis. f
52

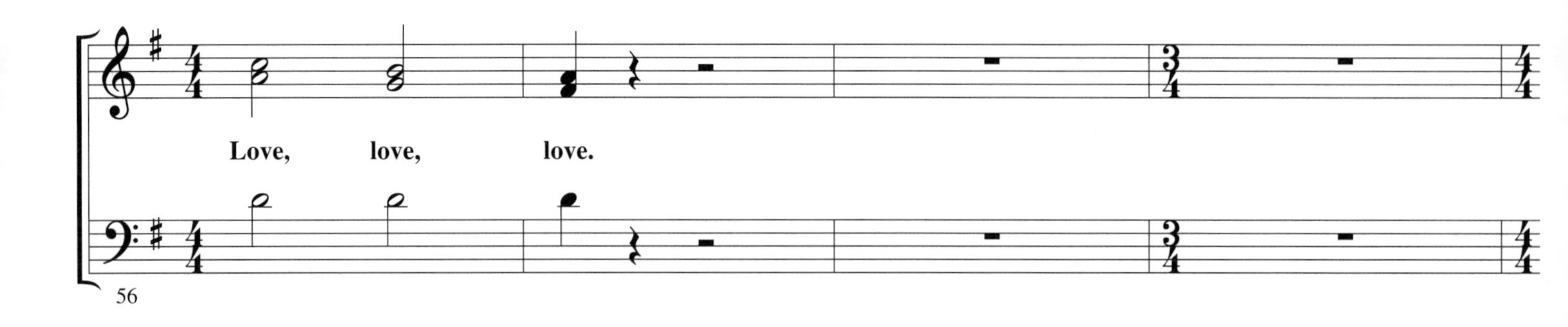
Love, love, love.
56

Unis.
All you need is love. All you need is love.
60

All you need is love, love;
63

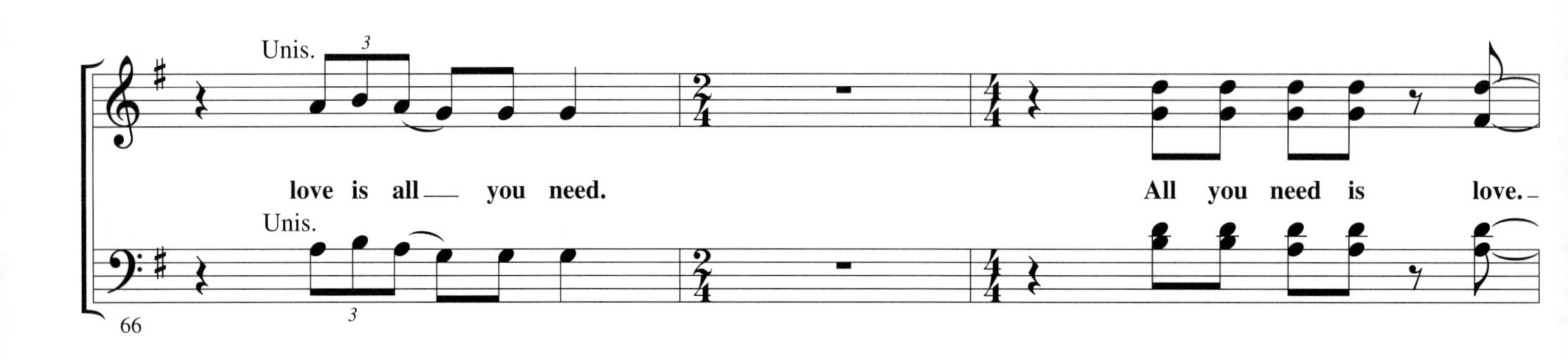
Unis.
love is all you need. All you need is love.
Unis.
66

Solo (male or female)
Solo (male or female)
All to - geth - er now!
All you need is love.
Ev - 'ry - bod - y!
69

All you need is love, love;
love is all you need.
72

Love is all you need.
All you need is love, love.
75

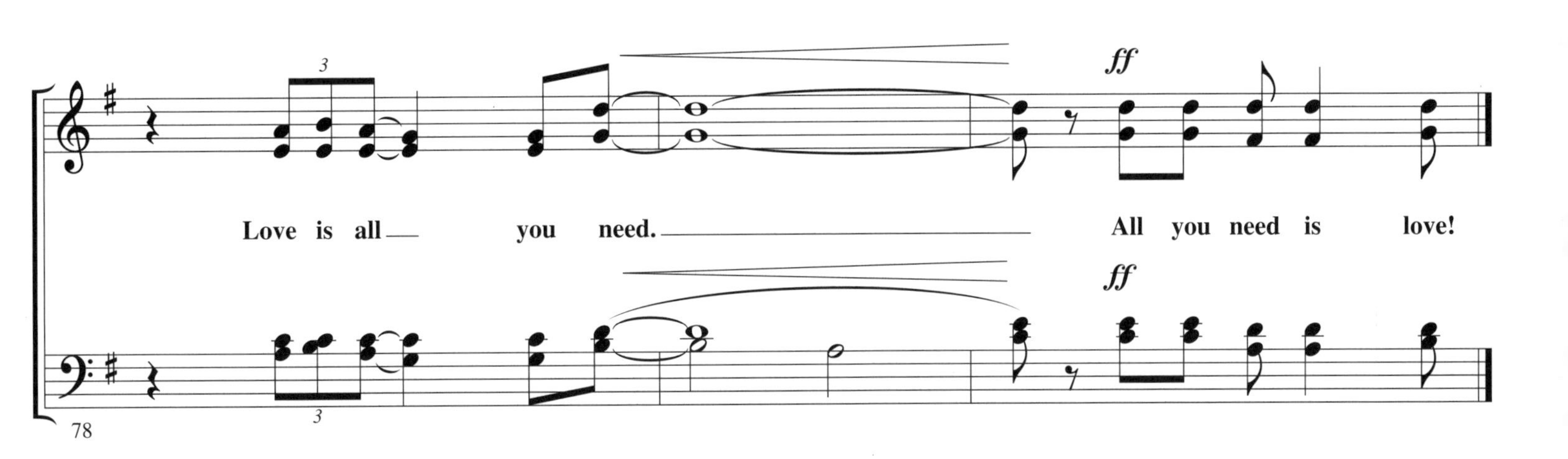
ff
Love is all you need.
All you need is love!
ff
78

At The Hop

Arranged by
ED LOJESKI

Words and Music by ARTHUR SINGER,
JOHN MADARA and DAVID WHITE

rec - ord starts a - spin - nin', you ca - lyp - so when you chick - en, at the hop.
Hop, hop, hop, hop. Hop, hop, hop, hop.
19
Do the dance sen - sa - tion that is sweep - in' the na - tion, at the
Ah, at the
22
hop.
(Let's go!)
f
Let's go to the hop!
f
(♮)
hop, hop, hop, hop.
Let's go to the hop!
25
Let's go to the hop!
(♮)
Oh, ba - by, Let's go to the hop! Oh, ba - by,
28
Let's go to the hop! Let's go to the hop!
(♮)
Let's go to the hop! Oh, ba - by, Let's go to the hop! Oh, ba - by,
31

ff
Ah,
Let's go to the hop!
(Let's go!)
ff
35
Ah,
f
Ah
f
39
Ah
43
Well, you can
mf
Oo
Ah.
47
swing it, you can groove it, you can real - ly start to move it, at the hop.
mf
Hop, hop, hop, hop.
Hop, hop, hop, hop.
mf
51

Where the jump - in' is the smooth - est and the mu - sic is the cool - est, at the
Hop, hop, hop, hop.
54
hop. All the cats and the chicks can
Hop, hop, hop, hop. Ah
57
get their kicks, at the hop. (Let's go!)
at the hop, hop, hop, hop.
60
f
Let's go to the hop! Let's go to the hop!
f
(♯)
63
Let's go to the hop! Oh, ba - by, Let's go to the hop!
Let's go to the hop!
66
Oh, ba - by, Let's go to the hop! Oh, ba - by,

Let's go to the hop!
Ah,
Let's go to the hop! Oh, ba - by,
69
Let's go to the hop!
72
ff Ah,
ff Ah,
Ah,
ff
Ah,
75
ff Ah,
Ah,
Ah,
Ah,
Ah,
Ah,
Ah,
78
Ah,
Ah, at the hop!
Ah, at the hop!
Ah,
at the hop!
81
Ah,
at the hop!

The Great Pretender

Arranged by
ROGER EMERSON

Words and Music by
BUCK RAM

need is such I pre - tend too much;
need is such I pre - tend too much;
need is such I pre - tend too_ much; I'm_
7
need is such I pre - tend too much;
lone - ly_ but no one can tell.
lone - ly_ but no one can tell.
lone - ly_ but no one can tell. Oh
9
lone - ly_ but no one can tell.
Yes, I'm the great pre - tend - er. A -
Yes, I'm the great pre - tend - er._ Oo wee oo wee oo,
yes, I'm the great pre - tend - er. A -
11
Yes, I'm the great pre - tend - er. A -

drift in a world of my own. I
'drift in a world of my own. Oo wee oo wee oo,
drift in a world of my own. I
drift in a world of my own. I
13
play the game but to my real shame
play the game but to my real shame
play the game but to my real shame you've
play the game but to my real shame
15
left me to grieve all a - lone.
left me to grieve all a - lone.
left me to grieve all a - lone. Too
left me to grieve all a - lone.
17

Too real is this feel - ing of make believe;
Too real is this feel - ing of make Oo wee oo wee oo;
real is this feel - ing of make be-lieve; Too
Too real is this feel - ing of make be-lieve;
19
Too real when I feel what my heart can't con-ceal. Woh
Too real when I feel what my heart can't con-ceal. Woh
real when I feel what my heart can't con-ceal. Woh
Too real when I feel what my heart can't con-ceal. Woh
21
Yes, I'm the great pre-tend - er. Just
Yes, I'm the great pre-tend - er. Oo wee oo wee oo,
Yes, I'm the great pre - tend - er. Just
Yes, I'm the great pre-tend - er. Just
23

laugh - ing a - way like a clown. I
laugh - ing a - way like a clown. Oo wee oo wee oo,
laugh - ing a - way like a clown. I
26
laugh - ing a - way like a clown. I
seem to be what I'm not you see; wear - ing my heart like a
seem to be what I'm not you see; wear - ing my heart like a
seem to be what I'm not you see; I'm wear - ing my heart like a
28
seem to be what I'm not you see; wear - ing my heart like a
crown. Oo wee oo we oo,
crown. Oo wee oo we oo,
crown. Pre - tend - ing that you're still a - round. Too
31
crown. Oo wee oo we oo,

Too real is this feel - ing of make be - lieve;
Too real when I feel what my
Too real is this feel - ing of make Oo wee oo wee oo,
Too real when I feel what my
real is this feel - ing of make be - lieve;
Too real when I feel what my
Too real is this feel - ing of make be - lieve;
Too real when I feel what my
34
heart can't con - ceal. Woh
cresc.
Woh
37
f
Yes, I'm the great pre - tend - er.
Just
Yes, I'm the great pre - tend - er. Oo wee oo wee oo,
40

laugh - ing a - way like a clown. I seem to be what I'm
laugh - ing a - way like a clown. Oo wee oo wee oo, seem to be what I'm
laugh - ing a - way like a clown. I seem to be what I'm
42
laugh - ing a - way like a clown. I seem to be what I'm
molto rit.
not you see; wear - ing my heart like a crown.
molto rit.
not you see; wear - ing my heart like a crown.
molto rit.
not you see; I'm wear - ing my heart like a crown. Pre -
molto rit.
45
not you see; wear - ing my heart like a crown.
Slowly
rit. al fine
Still a - round.
rit. al fine
Still a - round.
rit. al fine
tend - ing that you're still a - round.
rit. al fine
div.
48
Still a - round.

Good Vibrations

Arranged by
ED LOJESKI

Words and Music by BRIAN WILSON
and MIKE LOVE

Altos only
div.
f
Good, bop, bop, good vi - bra -
add Tenors
f
Bass
23
I'm pick - ing up good vi - bra - tions.

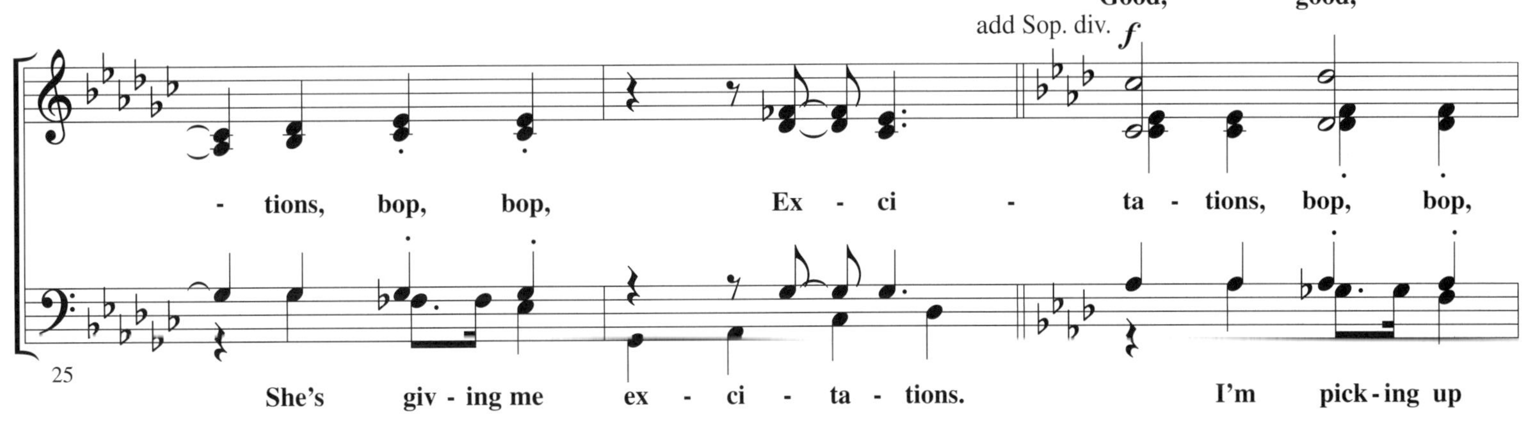
Good, good,
add Sop. div.
f
- tions, bop, bop, Ex - ci - ta - tions, bop, bop,
25
She's giv - ing me ex - ci - ta - tions. I'm pick-ing up

good, good vi - bra - tions.
To Coda
good vi - bra - tions, bop, bop. Ex - ci -
ff
28
good vi - bra - tions. She's giv - ing me ex - ci - ta - tions.

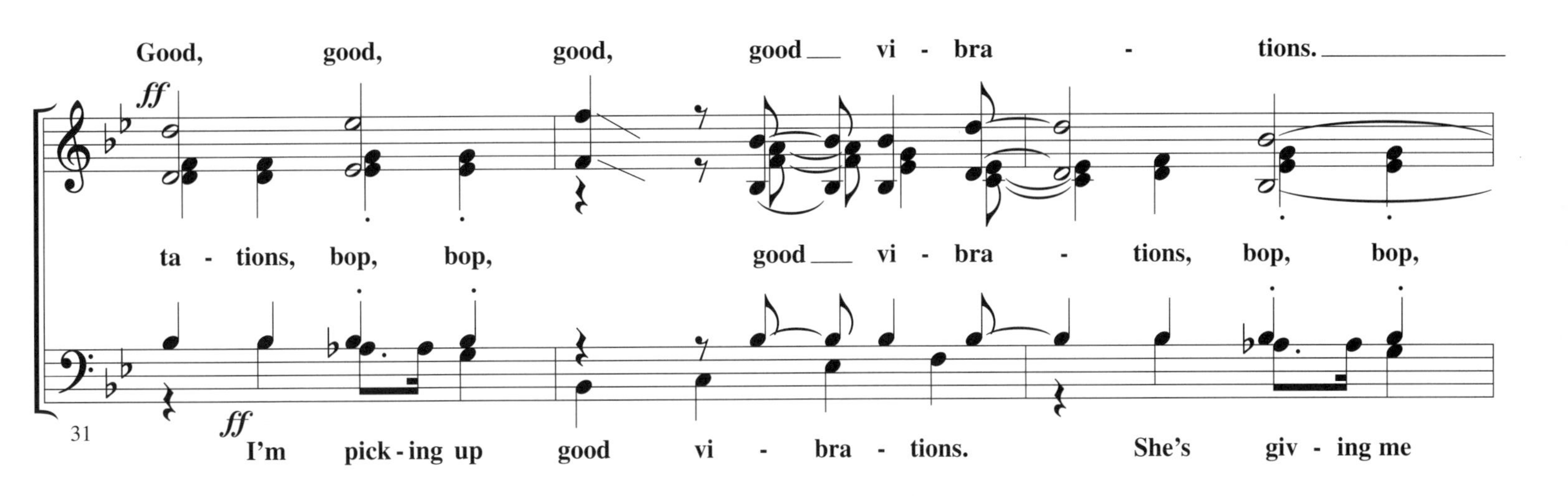
Good, good, good, good vi - bra - tions.
ff
ta - tions, bop, bop, good vi - bra - tions, bop, bop,
31
ff
I'm pick-ing up good vi - bra - tions. She's giv - ing me

p
Ex - ci - ta - tions.
Tenor
Solo
p
34
ex - ci - ta - tions. Close my eyes, she's some - how
37
clos - er now. Soft - ly smile, I
40
know she must be kind.
mp
43
Then I look in her eyes.
End Solo
D.S. al Coda
2
46
She goes with me to a blos - som world.

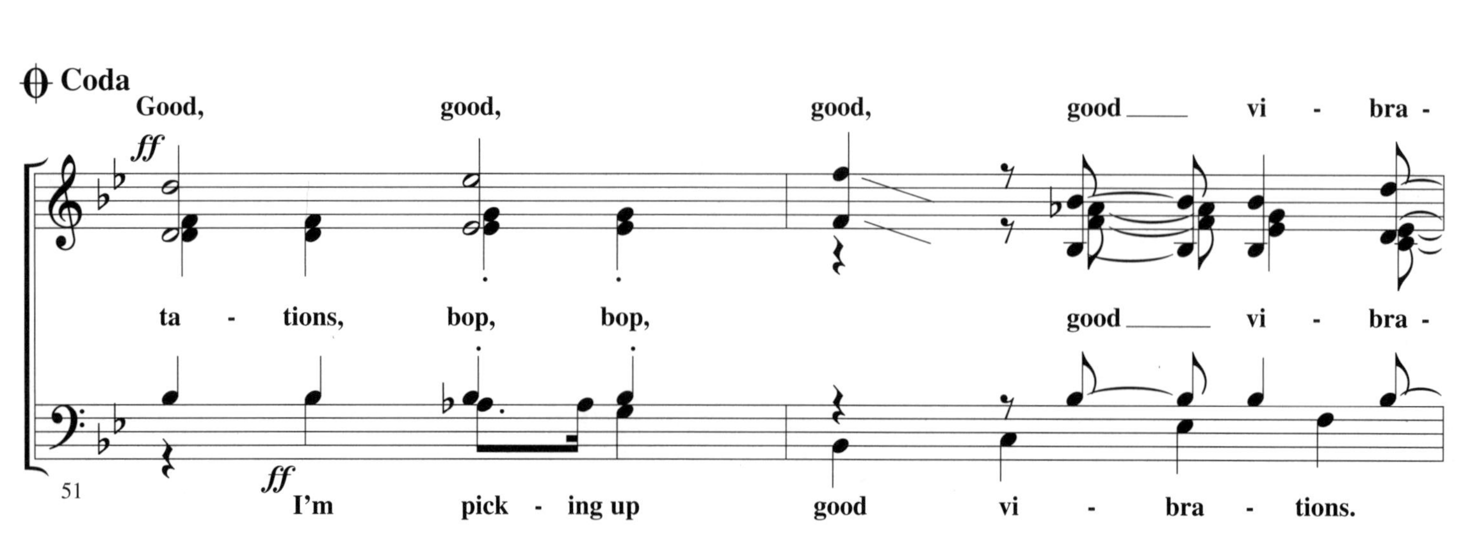
Coda
Good, good, good, good vi - bra -
ff
ta - tions, bop, bop, good vi - bra -
ff
51
I'm pick - ing up good vi - bra - tions.

tions.
tions, bop, bop. Ex - ci -
53
She's giv - ing me ex - ci - ta - tions.

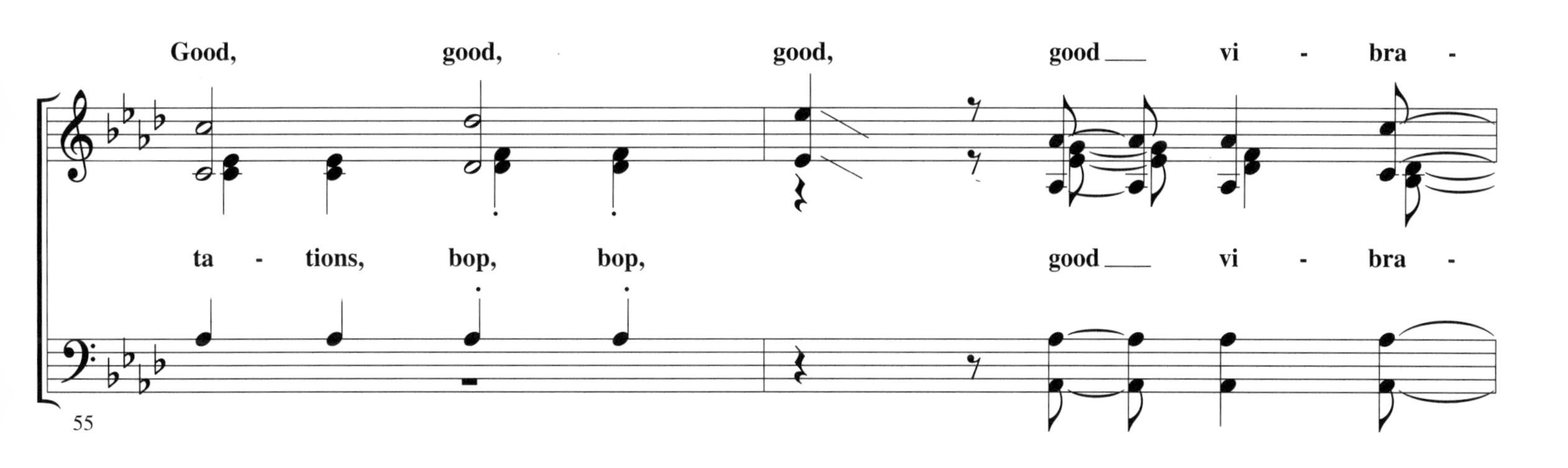
Good, good, good, good vi - bra -
ta - tions, bop, bop, good vi - bra -
55

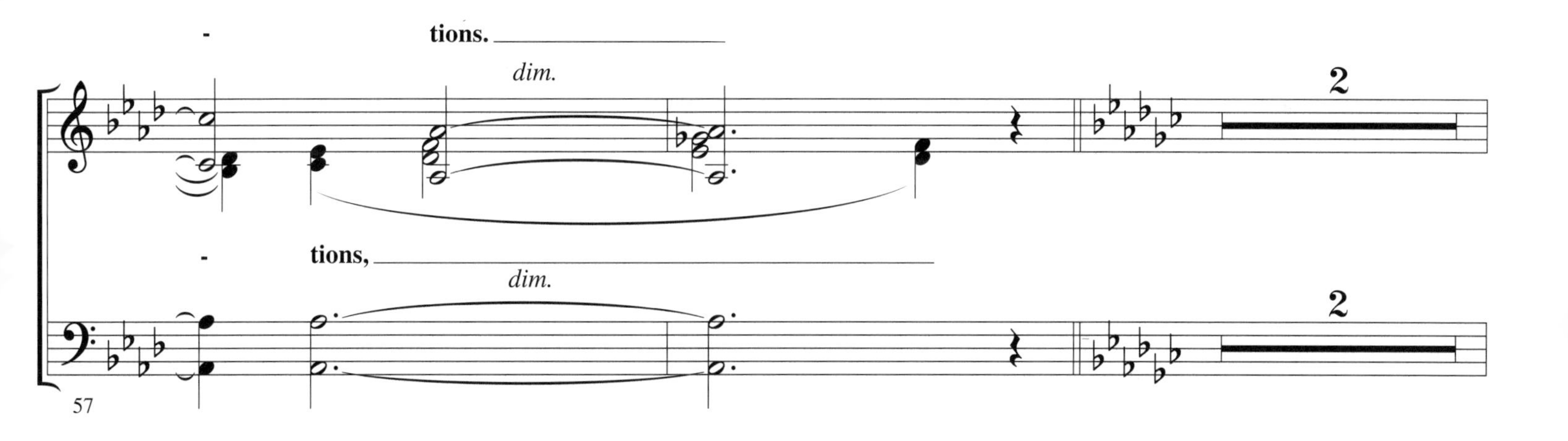
tions.
dim.
tions,
dim.
2
2
57

Sop. only
mf
La da, da, da, da, da, da, da. La da, da, da, da,
Basses only mf
61
Dot, dot, da,

La, da, da, da, da, da, da, da.
da, da, da.
add Altos mf
Da, da, da, da, da.
Dot, dot.
add Tenors
mf
64
da.
Da, da, da, da, da, da.
La, da, da, da, da, da, da, da.
Da, da, da, da, da.
Dot, da
dot, dot.
67
Da, da, da, da, da, da.
ff
Good, good,
div.
Ah
Good, bop, bop,
ff
70
I'm pick - ing up
good, good vi - bra - tions.
good vi - bra - tions, bop, bop. Ex - ci -
73
good vi - bra - tions. She's giv - ing me ex - ci - ta - tions.

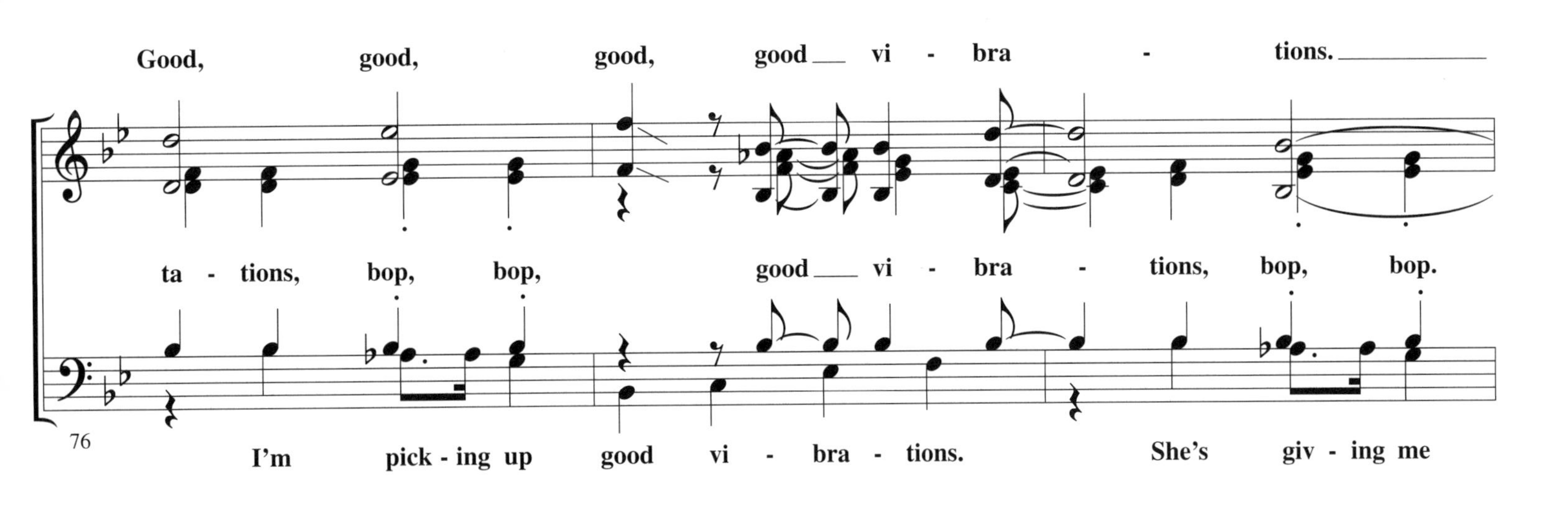
Good, good, good, good vi - bra - tions.
ta - tions, bop, bop, good vi - bra - tions, bop, bop.
76
I'm pick - ing up good vi - bra - tions. She's giv - ing me

Good, good, good, good vi - bra -
Ex - ci - ta - tions, bop, bop, good vi - bra -
79
ex - ci - ta - tions. I'm pick - ing up good vi - bra - tions.

- tions.
fff
- tions, bop, bop. Ex - ci - ta - tions.
fff
82
She's giv - ing me ex - ci, ex - ci - ta - tions.

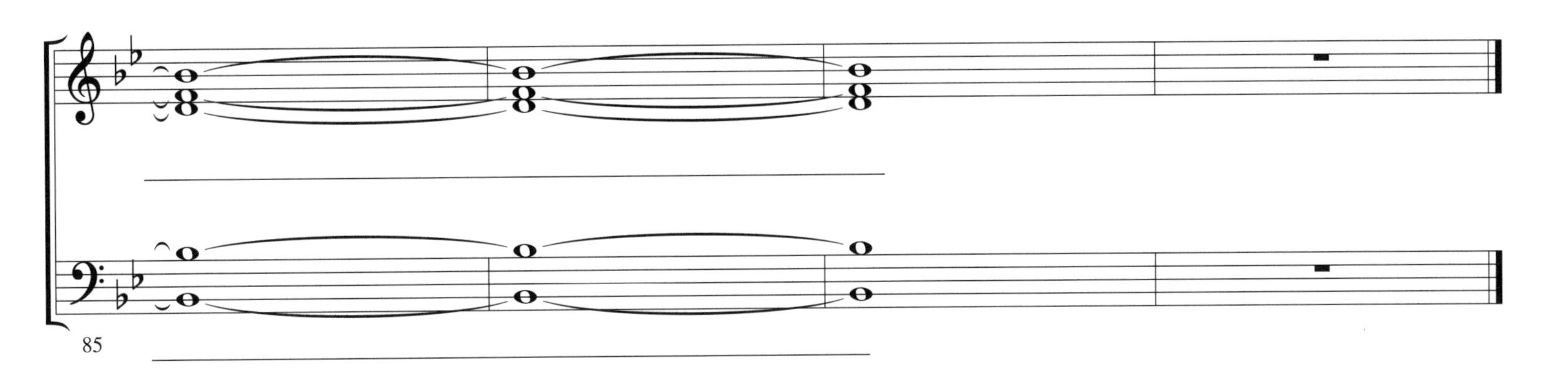
85

I'm A Believer

Arranged by
MARK BRYMER

Words and Music by
NEIL DIAMOND

me.
That's the way it seemed.
Dis - ap - point - ment haunt - ed all my dreams.
Then I saw her face.
Now I'm a be - liev - er.
Unis.
Not a trace
of doubt in my mind.
I'm in love.
16
19
22
25
28

I'm a be - liev - er. I could - n't leave
Oo, ah.
31
Unis.
To Coda
her if I tried.
Unis.
34
mf
I thought love was more or less a giv - in' thing,
mf
37
but the more I gave, the less I
40
got.
What's the use in try -
Oh,
43

- ing?
All you get is pain.
oh,
46
When I want - ed sun - shine, I got rain.
oh.
49
f
D.S. al Coda
Then I saw her face.
51
Coda
9
Then I saw her face.
53
Now I'm a be - liev -
63

- er.
Not a trace
of doubt in my mind.
Unis.
I'm in love.
I'm a be - liev - er.
Unis.
I be - lieve, I be - lieve, I be - lieve, I be - lieve, I be -
lieve, I be - lieve, I'm a be - liev - er!
65
68
71
74
76

ff
ff
div.
I be - lieve, I'm a be - liev -
78
- er!
I be -
81
I be - lieve!
div.
lieve, I'm a be - liev - er!
84
I be - lieve!
div.
I be - lieve!
87

Imagine

Arranged by
MAC HUFF

Words and Music by
JOHN LENNON

Im-ag-ine there's no coun - tries.
It is-n't hard to do.
Oo
Oo
17
Noth-ing to kill or die for
and no re-li-gion too.
Oo
Oo
21
mp cresc.
Im - ag - ine all the peo - ple
liv - ing life in peace.
Unis. mp cresc.
Unis.
25
mp
Unis.
You
you may say
I'm a dream-er.
Unis. mp
28
But I'm not the on - ly one.
cresc.
I hope some - day you'll
cresc.
31

join us
and the world will be as one.
34
Unis.
Will be as one. One.
Unis. f
Im - ag - ine no pos - ses -
37
- sions.
I won - der if you can.
41
No need for greed or hun - ger,
a broth - er - hood of man.
44
Im - ag - ine all the peo - ple
47

mf
Unis.
shar - ing all the world. You, you may say I'm a
Unis.
mf
50
dream - er But I'm not the on - ly one.
53
dim.
rit.
I hope some - day you'll join us and the world will
56
be as one, will be as one,
p
be as one, one.
be as one, be as one,
p
59
be as one,

Rock Around The Clock

Arranged by
ROGER EMERSON

Words and Music by MAX C. FREEDMAN
and JIMMY DeKNIGHT

clock strikes one. We're gon - na rock a - round the clock to - night, we're gon - na
12
rock, rock, rock, 'til the broad day - light. Gon - na
15
Unis.
rock, gon - na rock a - round the clock to - night!
17
When the clock strikes two, three and four if the
When it's eight, nine, ten, 'lev - en, too, I'll be
Unis.
20
band slows down we'll yell for more. We're gon - na
go - in' strong and so will you. We're gon - na
23

rock a - round the clock to - night, we're gon - na
25
rock, rock, rock, 'til the broad day - light. Gon - na
27
Unis.
rock, gon - na rock a - round the clock to - night!
29
To Coda
"Dance Break"
10
Unis.
When the
10
Unis.
32
D.S. al Coda
chimes ring five, six and sev - en, we'll be right in sev - enth hea - ven. Gon - na
45

Coda
ff Unis.
When the clock strikes twelve we'll
ff Unis.
49
pool our friends, start a rock - in' 'round the clock a - gain. We're gon - na
52
Unis.
rock a - round the clock to - night! We're gon - na rock, rock, rock, 'til the
55
Unis.
broad day - light. Gon - na rock, gon - na rock a - round the clock to - night!
58
opt. div.
opt. shake
Yeah!
61

Under The Boardwalk

Arranged by
MAC HUFF

Words and Music by ARTIE RESNICK
and KENNY YOUNG

* All low F's in bass may be sung 1 octave higher.

16
And your shoes get so hot you wish your tired feet were fire-
19
-proof.
Un-der the Board-walk,
Unis.
22
down by the sea,
Unis.
yeah,
on a
Unis.
To Coda
25
blan-ket with my ba-by, that's where I'll be.
Oo
28
From the park you hear the hap-py sound of a car-rou-sel.
Oo

Oo
You can al - most taste the hot
31
Oo
D.S. al Coda
dogs and French fries they sell.
Un - der the Board -
Unis.
34
Coda
be.
Out
37
Un - der the Board - walk,
of the sun,
we'll be hav - in' some fun,
40
un - der the Board - walk,
un - der the
peo - ple walk - in' a - bove,
we'll be
43
Board - walk,
un - der the Board - walk,

fall - in' in love under the Board - walk, Board - walk.
un - der the
46
Oo Oh
mp
Unis.
Oo Oh doo doo doo
Bm bm bm bm bm bm Bm bm bm bm
49
Oo La la la la la la la la
bm bm bm bm bm bm bm bm
52
la Un - der the Board - walk,
Unis.
55
Unis.
down by the sea, yeah. On a
Unis.
58

blan-ket with my ba-by, that's where I'll be.
61

out of the sun,
64
Un-der the Board - walk, un-der the

we'll be hav-in' some fun, peo-ple
67
Board - walk, un-der the Board - walk,

walk-in' a - bove, we'll be fall-in' in love un-der the
70
un-der the Board-walk. Un-der the

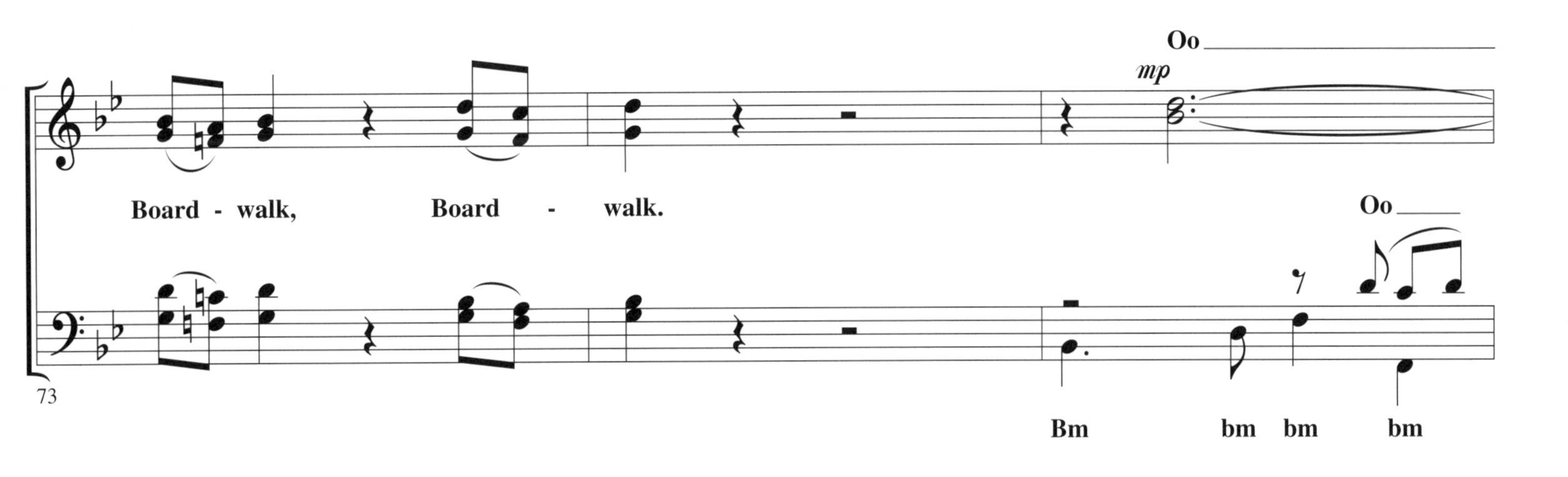
Oo
mp
Board - walk,
Board - walk.
Oo
73
Bm
bm
bm
bm

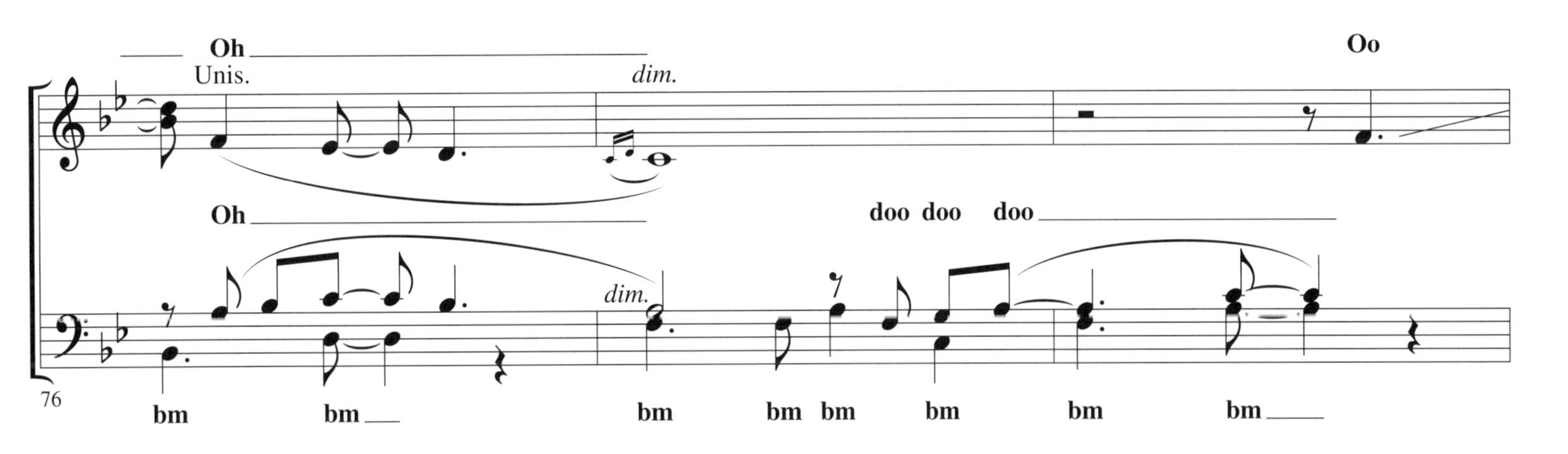
Oh
Unis.
dim.
Oo
Oh
doo doo doo
dim.
76
bm
bm
bm
bm bm
bm
bm
bm

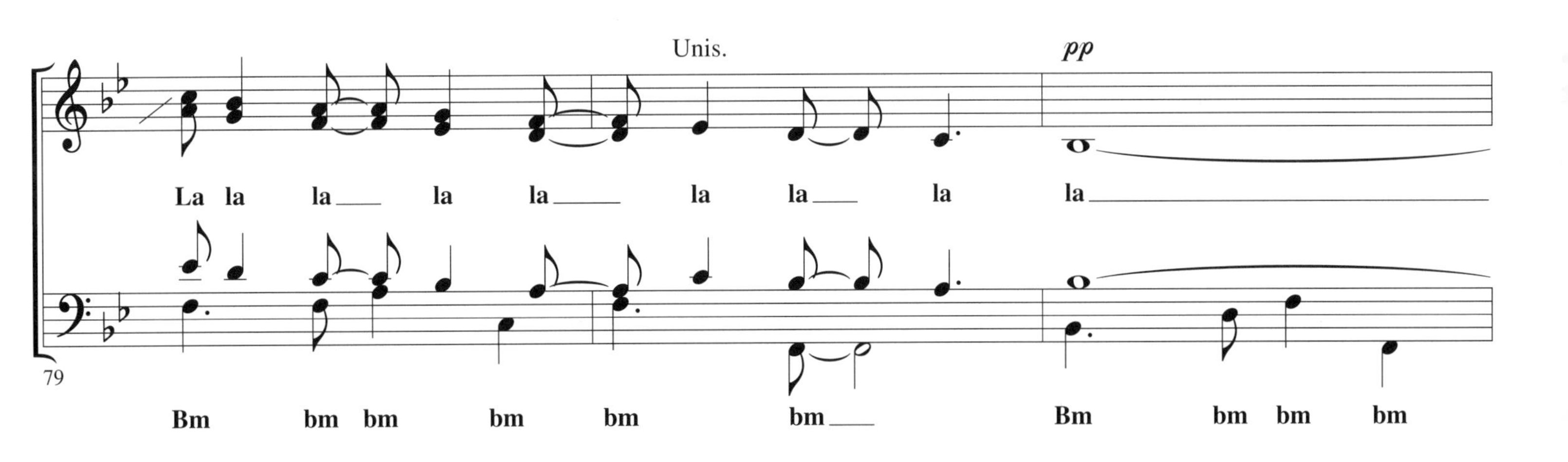
Unis.
pp
La la la la la la la la la
79
Bm bm bm bm bm bm
Bm bm bm bm

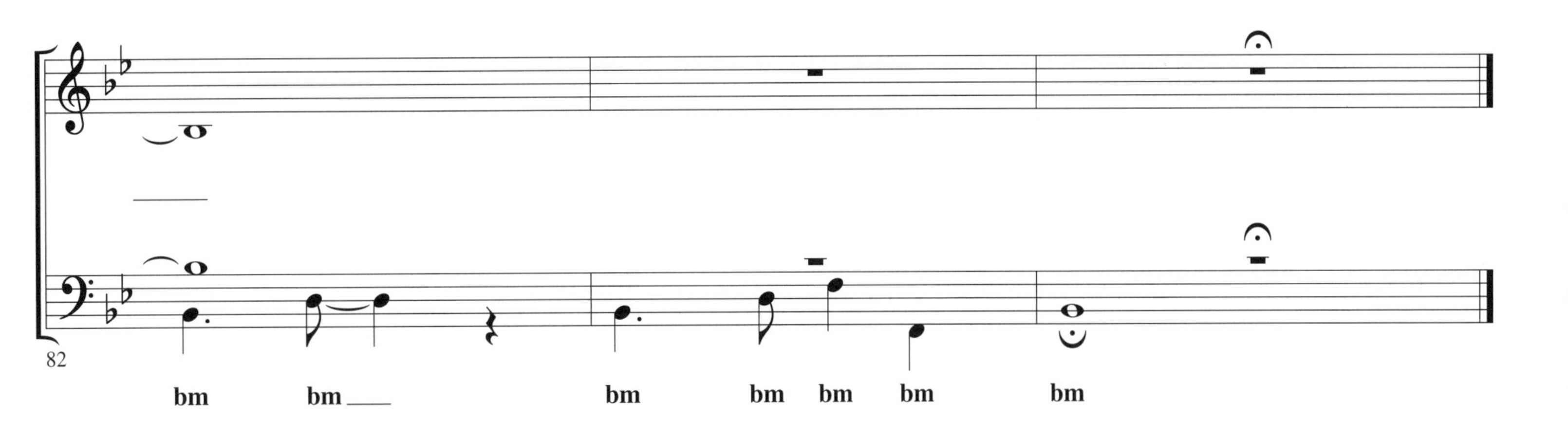
82
bm bm bm bm bm bm bm